W9-CLA-836

Monica and the School Spirit Meltdown

by Diana G. Gallagher

STONE ARCH BOOKS
a capstone imprint

Monica is published by Stone Arch Books
A Capstone Imprint
151 Good Counsel Drive, P.O. Box 669
Mankato, Minnesota 56002
www.capstonepub.com

Printed in the United States of America in Stevens Point, Wisconsin.
032010
005741WZF10

Library of Congress Cataloging-in-Publication Data is available on the Library of Congress website.

Library binding: 978-1-4342-1983-1

Summary: Monica is torn between rooting for her school's football team and the team that her friend Rory plays for. Things get complicated when she is asked to be a substitute rider in the rival team's parade.

Art Director/Graphic Designer: Kay Fraser
Production Specialist: Michelle Biedscheid

Photo credits:
Cover: Delaney Photography
Avatars: Delaney Photography (Claudia), Shutterstock: Aija Avotina (guitar), Alex Staroseltsev (baseball), Andrii Muzyka (bowling ball), Anton9 (reptile), bsites (hat), debra hughes (tree), Dietmar Höpfl (lightning), Dr_Flash (Earth), Elaine Barker (star), Ivelin Radkov (money), Michael D Brown (smiley face), Mikhail (horse), originalpunkt (paintbrushes), pixel-pets (dog), R. Gino Santa Maria (football), Ruth Black (cupcake), Shvaygert Ekaterina (horseshoe), SPYDER (crown), Tischenko Irina (flower), VectorZilla (clown), Volkova Anna (heart), Capstone Studio: Karon Dubke (horse Monica, horse Chloe)

{ table of contents }

FRIEND BOOK

Wall | Pictures

WELCOME BACK, MONICA MURRAY SCREEN NAME: MonicaLuvsHorses

YOUR AVATAR PICTURE

All updates from your friends

ADAM LOCKE is getting ready for the big game by stuffing my face with spaghetti and meatballs.

CLAUDIA CORTEZ has invited you to an event: Make Cougars Buttons! Where? Claudia's house. When? Monday after school. What? Make buttons supporting the best football team around, the Pine Tree Cougars!!!

BECCA MCDOUGAL: Count me in! Go Cougars!

RORY WEBER shared a link: from Rock Creek Babbler "Arch-Rivals Pine Tree and Rock Creek Battle in Seventh-Grade Match-up"

BECCA MCDOUGAL voted PINE TREE COUGARS in the poll, "Who do you think will win the big game on Saturday?"

CHLOE GRANGER has updated her information. She added "The Rock Creek Riders" to her activities.

TOMMY PATTERSON to BECCA MCDOUGAL: You're going to the game, right? We should sit together. :)

OWEN HARGROVE III has updated his information. He added "Honor lies in the mane of a horse. ~Herman Melville" to his favorite quotes.

CLAUDIA CORTEZ got all the button supplies today! Already thinking of awesome slogans...

BECCA MCDOUGAL to TOMMY PATTERSON: Of course I am! See you there. :)

ANGELA GREGORY scored 35,000 points in CHEERLEADER TRYOUT BLAST.

ANNA DUNLAP can't wait to cheer at the biggest football game of the year. Give me a C! Give me an O! Give me a U! Give me a G! Give me an A! Give me an R! Give me an S! What's that spell??? COUGARS COUGARS GOOOOOOOOO COUGARS!

Carly Madison likes this.

CHLOE GRANGER voted ROCK CREEK BEARS in the poll, "Who do you think will win the big game on Saturday?"

PETER WIGGINS has computed the odds and believes that Rock Creek will LOSE the game.

Tommy Patterson likes this.

FRANK JONES will be accompanying his granddaughters to the big game this Saturday!

CLAUDIA CORTEZ and 10 other people have become fans of the Pine Tree Cougars.

CHLOE GRANGER and 10 other people have become fans of the Rock Creek Bears.

MONICA MURRAY feels torn . . .

Horses4Chloe said:
Be at the barn, ready to ride, at 3:30!

MonicaLuvsHorses said:
Why?

Horses4Chloe said:
Super surprise. You're going to love it!!!!!!!!

Chapter One

The Opposite of the Poem

"Monica, you promised!" Angela shrieked.

I sighed.

Most of the second-grade girls I knew were just like the poem: Sugar and spice and everything nice.

Not my stepsister. She was selfish, bossy, and loud. Nobody wrote any poems about her.

"Something came up," I told her. I sat down on my bed and reached for my boots. "We can make friendship bracelets tomorrow."

"I need them today!" Angela yelled. She stamped her foot. Then she put her hands on her hips and glared at me.

Our dog stretched out on the bed and yawned. Angela's fits didn't bother Buttons, but they really bothered me.

I was the one who had to put up with her tantrums and bad moods. Mom made that perfectly clear when she married Logan Gregory, Angela's father, two years ago.

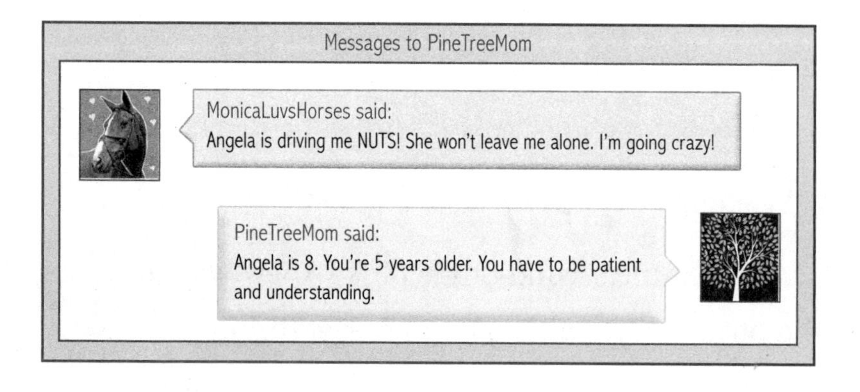

Angela just turned eight. She thought she was the center of the universe.

No matter how hard I tried, I couldn't keep her happy. And sometimes I just didn't feel like making her happy. Sometimes, things I liked were more important.

Like today.

I didn't know what was going on at the stable, but it had to be more exciting than stringing beads with my spoiled stepsister.

I never passed up a chance to ride. I was not going to miss it to make dumb bracelets with Angela.

"Everybody's bringing bracelets to school tomorrow! Now I won't have any, and it's your fault." Angela looked really mad.

"I'm sure Grandpa will help you," I told her. I finished pulling on my boots and stood up. "Come on, let's ask him."

"He's old, and you promised," Angela growled. Then she stomped into the kitchen behind me.

Grandpa was sitting at the kitchen counter, looking through a stack of mail.

"I have to go to the barn," I told Grandpa. "Can you watch Angela?

"Monica can't leave. I want her to make bracelets." Angela's lower lip quivered.

"I can make bracelets," Grandpa said.

"But Monica promised!" Angela cried.

"We'll do something extra special together on Wednesday," I said.

"Like what?" Angela asked.

"I don't know, but it'll be good," I promised.

"As good as princess dress-up?" Angela asked.

"Better," I said.

Anything would be better than playing princess dress-up, honestly. I would rather eat mud than play princess with Angela. She was bossier than Anna Dunlap, the most popular — and the bossiest — girl at Pine Tree Middle School.

"What if you want to do something else on Wednesday?" Angela asked.

"I won't," I said.

I already knew Logan and Mom were working on Wednesday afternoon, and Grandpa would be busy at the Senior Center.

I was stuck with Angela whether I liked it or not.

I hoped she'd think that it was extra special to take Buttons to the park.

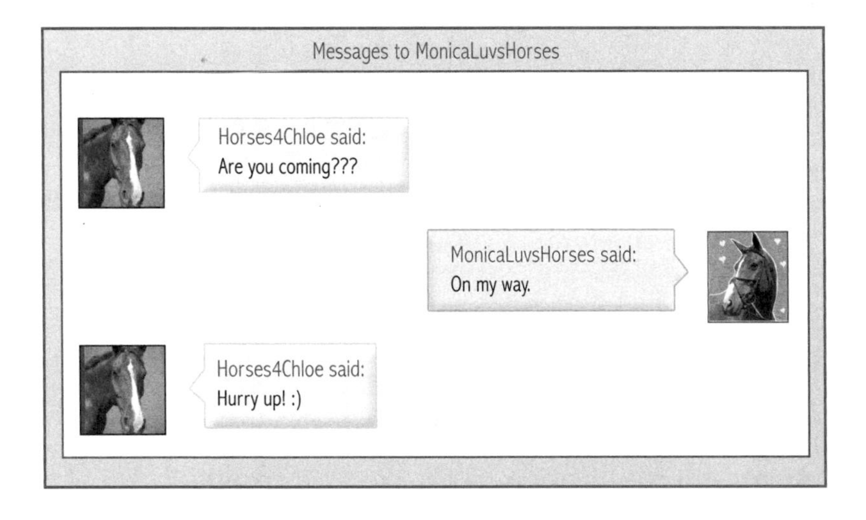

Chapter Two

One Horse Short

As I rode my bike to Rock Creek Stables, I couldn't stop wondering what Chloe's surprise was. I didn't think she could top her last secret surprise.

One day, she had asked me to meet her at the stables. When I got there, Chloe told me the news: her mother had decided I could ride her horse, Lancelot, whenever I wanted to. Dr. Granger was too busy to ride, and I didn't have a horse of my own.

There was no way Chloe's new surprise could beat that.

When I got to the stables, Chloe was sitting on a bench, waiting. She jumped up when I hopped off my bike.

"What's the big surprise?" I asked.

"Lydia has the flu," Chloe said. "We need you for drill team practice."

"You want me to be a Rock Creek Rider?!" I said. "For real?"

"Yeah!" Chloe said. "I'm so happy!"

I was thrilled.

I felt bad for Lydia, but I was really excited, too.

The drill team always got to go to special events. Now I was going to ride with them!

Megan Fitch and Owen Hargrove III, the leaders of the super-snotty stable crowd, were not thrilled, and they let me know it right away when they walked out of the barn together.

"You're not going to be a Rock Creek Rider, Monica," Megan said, leading her horse, Fine 'N' Dandy, out of the barn. "This is only until Lydia gets better."

"Lydia better be back by Friday," Owen said, frowning. He always looked like he had an upset stomach. Chloe called it his pickle face — but not when he could hear her. "We're riding in the Rock Creek Rally Parade."

"No Pine Tree spies allowed,"

Megan added.

The Rock Creek Bears and the Pine Tree Cougars were arch rivals. The teams were playing each other next Saturday. The winner would go on to play in the State Middle School Championship.

Owen wasn't the only one who hoped Lydia was better by Friday. I was the only kid at Rock Creek Stables who went to Pine Tree Middle School. I wanted to ride in a parade someday, but not in the Rock Creek football rally. It just felt wrong.

Alice, our instructor, helped Megan get on Dandy. Owen mounted his horse, Merlin. They joined the other riders in the arena. Then Alice came over to talk to me. "I hope you'll work with the team, Monica," she said. "We need twelve riders."

"I'd love to!" I told her. I was born horse crazy, and I wanted to be a great rider. I could learn a lot from the drill team.

"I've already saddled Rick-Rack and Lancelot," Chloe said.

I was excited, but suddenly, my happy bubble burst. The drill team rode in neat rows and performed fancy patterns. I didn't know what to do!

"What if I mess up?" I asked.

"Everybody messes up. That's why we practice," Alice said. She smiled, and I relaxed.

"Don't worry," Chloe said as we walked into the barn. "I've ridden Lancelot at drill team practice before. He never gives me any trouble."

Lancelot and I were on the end next to Chloe and Rick-Rack. First we practiced basic parade formation: four horses across in three lines.

It started off just fine. I was okay when we walked forward, but turning was tricky.

The horses were supposed to stay in a straight line when we turned a corner. That meant that the inside horse hardly moved. The second horse walked. The third horse trotted slowly. The fourth horse trotted faster. The rider had to pay close attention to what was going on. It was hard for me to figure out.

When we turned at the end of the arena, Lancelot didn't trot fast enough. The girl behind me, Jennifer, almost ran into us on her horse.

"Move, Monica!"

Jennifer yelled.

I kicked. Then Lancelot took off running! He ran to the other end of the ring before I could stop him.

I could feel my face getting hot. Right away, it was pretty obvious that Megan and Owen were annoyed.

"This is worse than being one horse short," Megan said, shaking her head. "Monica doesn't get it."

"Your horse isn't perfect either, Megan," Chloe said. "You have to be in the middle because Dandy gets jittery on the end."

"At least Dandy stays in line," Megan shot back. She frowned at me and Lancelot. "And I carry a flag."

"This is a drill team," Alice reminded everyone. "You have to work together."

Rory rode up to Alice. The two of them talked for a minute. Then Alice waved me over. "Rory is going to teach you the basics," she told me. "Then you won't have to worry as much about what you're doing."

"Okay," I said. "Thanks, Rory." I smiled, but I was embarrassed. I was mad at myself for not getting it right away.

"No problem. It's easy when you know what to do," Rory said. "Follow me."

As we rode away, I glanced at Chloe. She made a heart shape with her fingers. I rolled my eyes.

Chloe was sure that Rory had a crush on me. I was sure that Chloe was imagining things.

Rory was nice to everyone. It didn't mean he had a crush on me, and it didn't mean that I had to have a crush on him, either. Rory was just a nice guy.

He also knew a lot about horses! After Rory helped me for ten minutes, I could make Lancelot turn in a tight circle. I learned to squeeze my legs to make him go faster. When we joined the group again, Lancelot and I did all the turns perfectly!

"I guess that was better," Megan said when we were done. "But you're still not exactly Rock Creek Rider material."

I tried to ignore her.

The horse snobs at the stable — the ones who owned their own horses — were always mean to the kids like me who just came to the stable for lessons. That didn't mean that what they said was true. And anyway, Chloe thought I did a good job. Not all of the kids who owned their own horses were jerks.

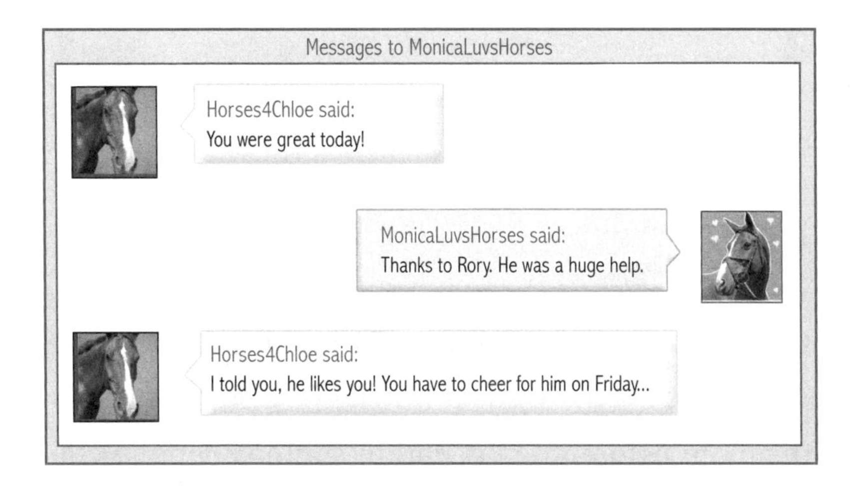

Rory was always friendly and helpful. I wanted to root for him in the big play-off game. But I had to be loyal to my school and the Pine Tree Cougars.

I didn't know what to do.

Chapter Three

Tommy, the Button Billboard

The next day at lunch, my best friend, Claudia, was acting weird. She didn't say anything to me while we waited in line with our other best friend, Becca. When I asked her if she'd watched our favorite show the night before, she just sort of shrugged and asked Becca a question.

Something was up.

"Are you mad at me?" I asked when we sat down at our usual table.

"Sort of," Claudia admitted.

A shock ran through me. I felt horrible. "What did I do?" I asked.

"It's what you didn't do," said my other best friend, Becca, as she sat down next to Claudia. Our friends Peter, Tommy, and Adam put their trays down on the table too.

"You promised you'd come over and help make football buttons," Claudia said. "You didn't show up yesterday."

"Oh, right!" I slapped my forehead. "The Rock Creek drill team needed an extra rider, and I forgot. I'm really sorry."

Claudia looked at Becca and sighed. She said, "Horses. We should've known."

I smiled. "I'm sorry," I told them. "How did it go?"

"We made a lot of buttons," Becca said.

"And they came out great," Peter said. He pointed to his chest. He was wearing a round green button with gold letters.

The button read:

Go Gold! Go Green!
Cougars are the best team!

Adam's button was different.

Cougars are cool!

Claudia wore a button too.

Pine Tree Cougars are #1!

"Can I do anything to make up for it?" I asked, looking at Claudia.

"Yes!" Claudia said. She grinned. She never stayed mad. "You can help us sell the buttons," she told me. "Here. You can have this one."

Claudia gave me a button that read:

I'm A Cougar Fan!

She held out a shoebox full of buttons. I reached in and pulled a few more buttons out. They read:

Don't mess with a Cougar!

Cougars are Champions!

My Favorite Animal is a Cougar!

"Where did you get the sayings?" I asked, carefully returning the buttons to the box.

"Becca and I made them up," Claudia said.

"The printing looks fantastic," I said.

"We used Claudia's computer to design them," Becca said. "Then we printed them out and cut out the circles."

"Then we squashed the circles, a plastic cover, and the metal parts together in the machine," Claudia explained.

"After we sell all of them, we're going to buy cider and donuts," Becca said. "So we don't starve at the Pep Rally on Friday night."

Just then, Anna Dunlap marched through the cafeteria with her popular friends. They all had bunches of pom-poms and big yellow Cougar claws for sale. They chanted a Pine Tree cheer.

"Go Green! Go Gold!
Cougars, Cougars, fast and bold!
Go Gold! Go Green!
Cougars are the winning team!"

Everybody in the cafeteria whistled and cheered.

"Show some real team spirit!" Anna yelled. "Get pom-poms and claws to wave at the game!"

The whole school was excited about the play-off game, but only a few kids bought pom-poms or claws from the cheerleaders. Anna was selling the souvenirs for $15 each. I think everyone thought that was too expensive.

"We should be selling buttons right now," I said. "It's the perfect time."

"Yeah," Peter agreed. "Our buttons only cost a dollar. People might not have enough to buy the claws, but I'm positive that they'll have enough for buttons."

"Let's do it!"

Claudia said. She reached into her shoebox and then handed Becca and me each a small pile of buttons.

Tommy pinned six buttons to his shirt. "I'm a button billboard!" he said.

But just then, Anna and Carly stopped by our table. They looked down at us.

"Your homemade buttons are **really lame**," Anna said. "Nobody will buy them."

"Pom-poms and Cougar claws are cool," Carly said. "We just sold three sets."

"We can't take Cougar claws to class," I said. "They're big and clunky. And nobody wants to walk around the mall with pom-poms. You can wear buttons anywhere."

"Right!" Claudia said. She smiled and gave me a thumbs-up.

"They look cool, though," Becca said. She was always nice. Even to Anna Dunlap, queen of the bullies.

"I want one!" Larry Kyle yelled as he walked up waving a dollar bill.

"Cougar claws are fifteen dollars," Anna said. She was smiling, but only because she wanted Larry's money. She usually ignored him.

"I don't want a claw," Larry said, pushing past Anna. "I want a button."

"I do too," Sylvia Slother said, walking over to our table. She looked through the box. She couldn't decide which button she liked best, so she bought three.

We sold half the buttons in Claudia's shoebox before the bell rang and we had to hurry to get to class.

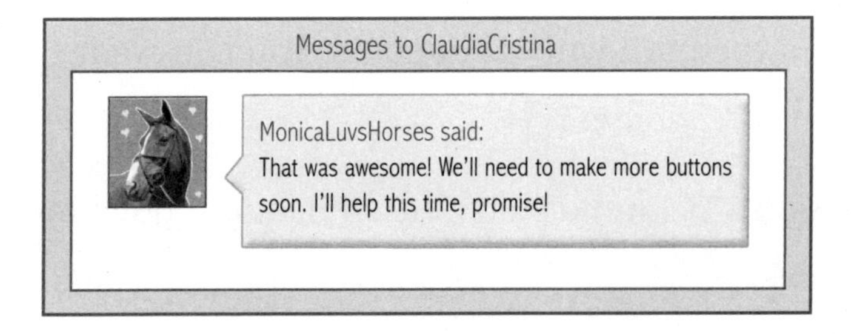

Chapter Four

Stable vs. School

Claudia, Becca, and I each took ten buttons to sell after school. I sold five to the waitresses at the Red Brick Inn where my mom works.

The waitresses wanted more. I promised I'd bring some back when I could.

Grandpa bought five buttons for his friends at the Senior Center. He gave me a five-dollar bill.

Just as I was putting the money into my pocket, Angela ran in.

"I want money!"

Angela yelled. She held out her hand.

"Grandpa is paying me for football buttons," I explained.

"I want a button!" Angela said. She climbed onto a stool.

"Which one do you like?" Grandpa asked. He put the buttons on the counter.

"I only like that one," Angela said. She pointed at the *I'm A Cougar Fan* button pinned to my shirt. I rolled my eyes.

Of course. Even with a bunch of other choices, the only button Angela wanted was mine.

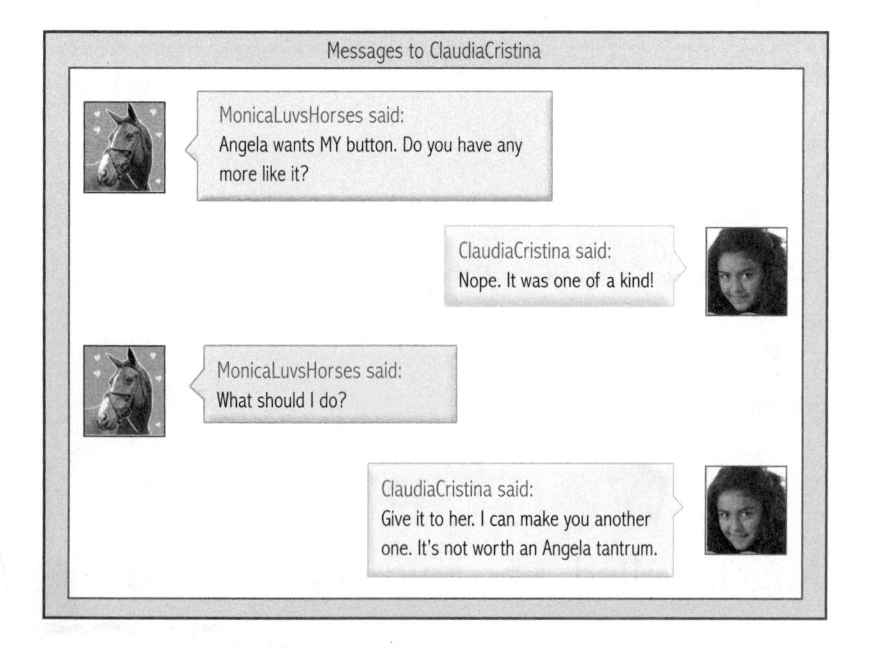

"What do you think, Monica?" Grandpa asked. "Can Angela have your button? I'll pay you for it."

I gave Angela my button.

"What's a fan?" Angela asked, pinning the button to her shirt.

"Someone who really, really, likes something," Grandpa said.

"Well, I really, really like the Cougars," Angela said. "They are my favorite team in the whole wide world! They're the best!"

"Since when do you like football?" I asked, narrowing my eyes. Something about this didn't add up. My stepsister had never acted interested in sports before in her life.

"Since Nick Wright wore a Cougar button to school today," Angela said dreamily.

Aha! No wonder Angela was suddenly interested in the Cougars.

Nick was the kid Claudia always got stuck babysitting. Angela had a huge crush on him. It was funny to watch Nick getting chased around by Angela, since Claudia and I were used to him annoying us.

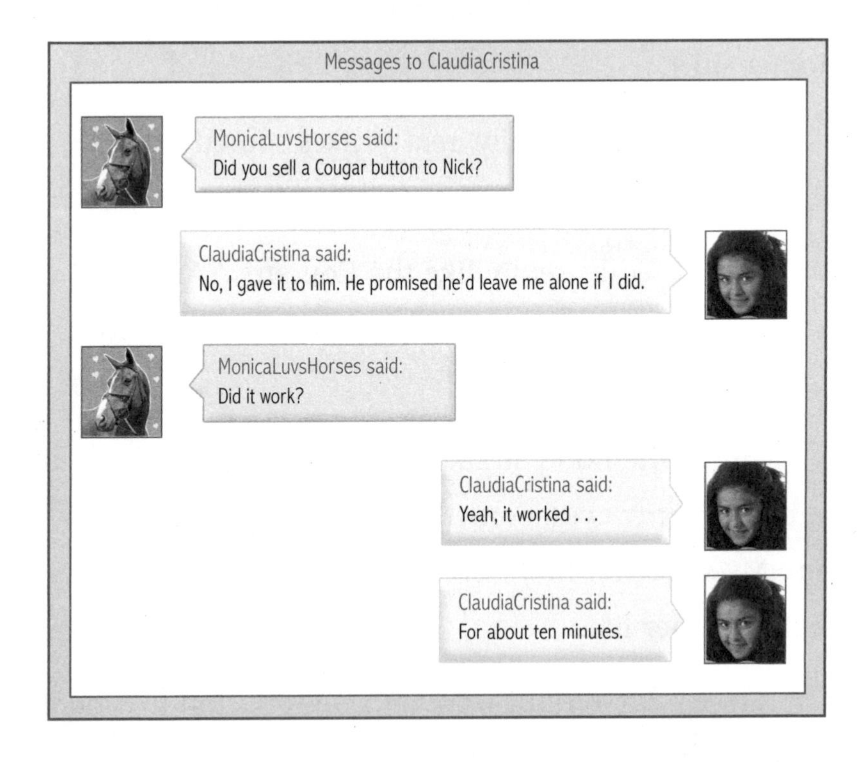

"All of the kids in my class want Cougar buttons," Angela told me. "They'll be so jealous of mine."

That gave me an idea. "If I can get you some buttons, will you sell them for me at school?" I asked Angela. "I'll let you keep half of the money you raise."

Angela looked thrilled. "Yes!" she said.

"Great," I told her. "I'll get you some tomorrow. Right now, I have to go to the barn."

Other Plans

I went to drill team practice without a button. Everyone at the barn knew I wanted the Cougars to win. I didn't want to rub it in.

"I'm so glad you're practicing with us," Chloe said as we rode to the arena. "Rick-Rack behaves better when he's with Lancelot."

"I just hope Lancelot doesn't run away again!" I laughed, but I was nervous when practice started. I got over it fast. Lancelot did all the turns exactly right.

Alice called us together at the end of practice. "Lydia will be back on Friday," she said.

That was great. Lydia had been in the drill team for a long time. She had put a lot of work into it, and she was a good rider. She deserved to ride in the Rock Creek Rally Parade.

But I was pretty disappointed. And so was Chloe. "I was hoping you could ride with us, Monica," she whispered. "Parades are fun."

"I'm glad Lydia's better," Rory told me. "But it's too bad you have to miss out. You worked hard."

"Maybe **next time**," I said.

"There won't be a next time," Megan said, narrowing her eyes at me. "You're not a Rock Creek Rider, Monica. Now that Lydia's going to be back, we don't need you anymore."

"This isn't the first time we've needed a substitute. All of you have missed practices," Alice said. "Dentist appointments and homework are important, but it's hard to train with eleven riders."

"Last year Megan missed our exhibition at the Brookville Horse Show," Chloe said.

"I had to go to a family reunion," Megan explained.

"Which was fine, but I had to ride in your place," Alice said. "We need a permanent substitute to be on the drill team."

"I nominate Monica Murray!" Rory shouted.

"I second it!" Chloe yelled, grinning. She and Rory slapped hands.

"All in favor?" Alice asked. She raised her hand.

One by one, everyone in the room raised their hands. Except Owen and Megan. Finally, they looked at each other, sighed, and raised their hands too. They would have looked like complete jerks if they didn't.

On the way back to the barn, Rory rode up beside me. "I'm glad you're officially on the drill team," he said. "Now you can come to the party Friday night."

"What party?" I asked.

"At Owen's house, after the parade," Chloe said.

Owen heard us and trotted over. "It's a party for the Rock Creek Bears," he said loudly. **"Monica can't come."**

Megan rode up next to us and added, "She goes to Pine Tree." She made the words Pine Tree sound like sour milk.

"That shouldn't matter," Chloe said.

"I can't come anyway," I said. "I have other plans."

I didn't tell them I was going to the Pine Tree Pep Rally on Friday night. And I definitely wasn't going to tell my Pine Tree friends that I was helping the Rock Creek Riders practice for their parade.

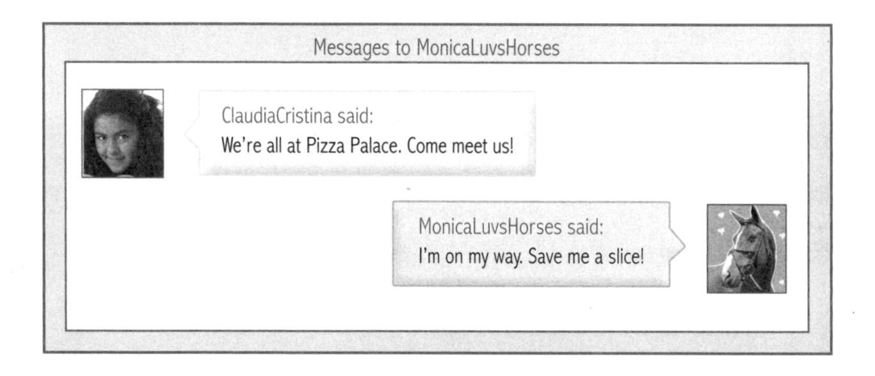

I went directly to Pizza Palace from the barn. Claudia, Becca, and the boys were waiting for me in our usual booth.

"Why aren't you wearing your Cougar button?" Tommy asked as I slid into the booth. He only had one button left on his shirt.

"Angela wanted it," I said.

Everyone nodded. They'd all met Angela. They knew about her tantrums. That was all they needed to hear.

"I sold the rest," I added.

"We sold ours, too," Becca said.

"Except the ones we're wearing, of course," Peter added.

"I could sell a lot more," I said. "The waitresses at my mom's work loved them, and Angela said all the kids in her class are going crazy for them. She wants to sell them at the elementary school."

"Three kids asked me for buttons on my way here," Becca said.

"Then we have to make more," Claudia said. She looked at me. "Can you come to my house tomorrow?"

I winced. The next day was Wednesday. Mom and Dad were working. Grandpa was playing bingo at the Senior Center. And I made a promise to my stepsister.

"Yes," I said, "but I have to bring Angela."

Chapter Six

Angela Hearts Nick

Angela didn't kick and scream when I told her we were going to Claudia's house. She loved hanging out with my friends. She skipped and bounced down the sidewalk.

"Can I have more buttons?" Angela asked.

"Sure," I said. Saying no would have been a big mistake. Angela could be annoying even when she was happy. But when she was in a bad mood, you didn't want to be anywhere near her.

"How do you make buttons?" Angela asked.

"With a special machine," I said.

"Can I do it?" Angela begged. "Please?"

"You'll have to ask Claudia," I said.

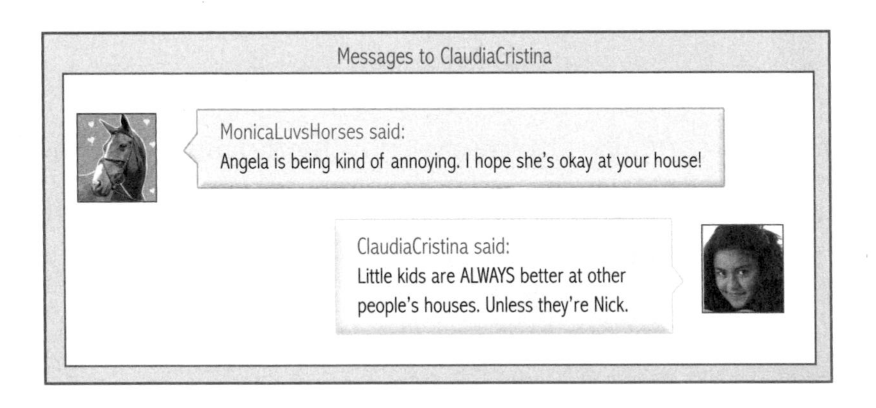

When we got to Claudia's house, the first thing Angela said was, "Can I make buttons?"

"Making buttons isn't easy," Claudia said. "You have to place the parts just right."

"Or the sayings come out crooked," Becca explained.

"Or the buttons fall apart," Claudia added.

"I can do it," Angela said.

"It's harder than it looks," Claudia said.

"We might as well let her try," Becca said.

"Can I get hurt making buttons?" Angela asked.

"The pins might stick you," Claudia said.

Angela shrugged. "I'll be careful," she told us.

Claudia showed her how to work the machine. Angela carefully put the parts in the machine. But she couldn't push the lever down. The pieces didn't squash together right.

She ruined five buttons. Then she got mad and gave up.

"Stupid machine!" Angela yelled. She sat on the sofa and pouted. "I'm bored."

"Do you want to cut out circles?" Becca asked. "That would be a big help."

"No," Angela said. She shook her head. "That sounds really boring."

"Would you like some cookies?" Claudia asked. "We have chocolate chip."

"I'm not hungry," Angela grumbled. She glared at the floor.

Angela didn't want to read *Teen Scene* or watch TV, either.

Sometimes I was positive that she liked being mad.

It always took her forever to get over it.

When Claudia's cat walked in, Angela perked up. She rushed over to pet the cat.

Ping-Ping ran away. Angela chased her, but the cat had lots of hiding places.

"Claudia's cat hates me!" Angela whined.

"Nick squirts her with the hose," Claudia explained. "She doesn't like little kids."

"I'm not a little kid!" Angela yelled.

Just then, Nick ran in. He skidded to a stop when he saw Angela.

"Nick!" Angela squealed. She stopped being mad about the cat and grinned.

Nick turned to leave, but it was too late to run. Angela grabbed his arm. "Let's watch TV," she said.

"Is *Cosmic Cadets* on?" Nick asked, yanking his arm free.

"I want to watch *Kidz,*" Angela said. She changed the channel to her show. Then she sat on the remote so Nick couldn't get it.

"That's a girl show!" Nick yelled. He bolted for the kitchen.

"Where are you going?" Angela asked, running after him.

Crash! Something in the kitchen fell to the floor.

Claudia, Becca, and I looked at each other. Then we ran into the kitchen.

Nick and Angela stood on opposite sides of the counter.

"Go away!" Nick growled. He tried to look mad and mean.

"I'm company," Angela said. "You have to play with me."

"No, I don't. I don't live here." Nick ran down the hall. He ducked into the bathroom and locked the door.

"Nick hates me!" Angela wailed. She marched down the hall and pounded on the bathroom door. "Come out right now!"

"No!" Nick shouted back.

I threw up my hands. My sister was running wild in Claudia's house. There was nothing I could do.

Becca shook her head. "I feel sorry for Nick."

"Me, too," Claudia agreed. "He's a brat, but at least he behaves when I bribe him."

"What does Angela like more than Nick?" Becca asked. "Maybe we can bribe her."

"Nothing," I said. "It's not worth trying. She's too stubborn to take a bribe."

"Maybe she can be distracted." Becca took a pair of Cougar pom-poms out of her backpack. "I'll try giving these to her."

"Did you buy those from Anna?" Claudia asked.

"No, from Carly," Becca said. "I really like them, and I wanted them for the game. Anyway, she promised to buy a button."

"Angela might like them," I said. I took the green and gold streamers from Becca. I shook the pom-poms and jumped up and down as I chanted a Pine Tree cheer:

"Go Pine Tree! Go team!
Go Cougars, gold and green!
Yay, Cougars!"

Angela ran into the room when she heard me cheering. She stared at me.

"Wow! That was great!" Claudia exclaimed when I was done.

"Do another one!" Becca said.

"Teach me!" Angela yelled. She jumped up and down in front of me. "I want to cheer."

"Okay, but we have to go outside," I told her. I handed the pom-poms back to Becca.

"We need those!" Angela whined. "I can't be a cheerleader without pom-poms!"

"All right," Becca said. "You can have them."

"Thanks!" Angela took the pom-poms and ran for the back door. "Come on, Monica!"

"I'll pay you back," I told Becca. Then I headed outside. It was pretty clear that I wasn't going to get to help make buttons after all.

Chapter Seven

No Grumpy Cheerleaders

By the time we were heading home, Angela had forgotten all about the buttons. She shook her pom-poms as we walked. "I'm going to be cheerleader when I'm in middle school," she told me.

"You can't just decide to be a cheerleader," I told her. "It doesn't work like that."

"Yes, I can," Angela said. "Daddy said I can be anything I want."

"You have to try out," I explained. "Some girls get picked and some don't."

"Oh, I'll get picked," Angela said.

I laughed. She was probably right.

"You will," I agreed. "Just remember three things: Learn the cheers, be super sweet, and smile."

"Even if I'm sick or mad?" Angela asked.

"There's no such thing as a grumpy cheerleader," I said.

We got home an hour before dinner. I went to my room to study. We were having a history quiz the next day, and I also wanted some time to myself.

My quiet time lasted ten minutes. Then Angela barged in. "Give me your Cougars t-shirt," she demanded.

"Why do you need my t-shirt?" I asked.

"For my cheerleading outfit," Angela said. "I have green shorts and white sneakers. I need a gold shirt."

"You have a yellow shirt," I reminded her.

"Yellow isn't gold," Angela said.

"My shirt is too big for you," I said.

"So?" Angela rolled her eyes.

I raised my eyebrows. "You're not smiling," I told her. "Cheerleaders always smile."

Angela faked a smile. Then she talked through gritted teeth. "Please, Monica, give me your Cougar t-shirt," she said.

I gave her a Cougars shirt I wore last year. It was a little faded, but Angela liked it. She was still happy when we sat down to dinner.

Mom didn't have to work, so she was there, too. So was Logan, my stepdad.

"Did everyone have a good day today?" Logan asked.

"I guess so," Grandpa grumbled. "Only three people showed up for the bingo tournament."

"Did you win?" Angela asked.

"Yes, but it was too easy," Grandpa told her. Then he looked at me. "By the way, I need twelve more Cougars buttons for the Senior Center."

"I've got them," I said. "How many do you want for the Red Brick Inn, Mom?"

"Ten," Mom said.

"I'll take the rest," Logan said. "Everyone at Granite Electric is cheering for the Cougars."

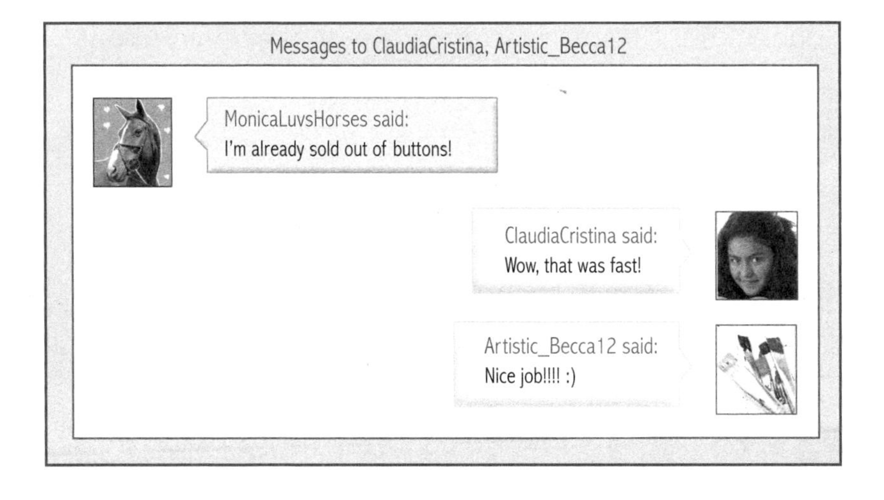

"I'm a Cougar fan too," Angela said, pointing at her button. She held out her plate and smiled. "No potatoes, please."

"You're in a really good mood, Angela," Mom said.

"Yes, I am!" Angela said.

"Did you have fun with Monica?" Logan asked.

"We went to Claudia's house. Nobody helped me make buttons, Nick didn't want to play with me, and I messed up," Angela said sadly. Then she grinned. "But Becca gave me pom-poms, and Monica taught me some cheers."

"That's **wonderful**," Logan said. He smiled at me. "Are you excited about the big game on Saturday, Monica?"

"I guess so," I said.

The truth was, I was having a hard time getting excited. I felt too torn about the game.

I wanted to cheer for Pine Tree. I just didn't want my Rock Creek friends to notice. I hoped the Cougars won, but I'd feel awful if the Bears lost. So I'd feel bad either way.

"I want to go to the game!" Angela exclaimed. "I'm a fan, and I know the cheers!"

"I'll take you," Grandpa said. "I love football."

"Oh, goody!" Angela bounced in her chair. "We can sit with Monica's friends!"

Mom, Logan, and Grandpa looked happy.

I smiled, but I was not happy.

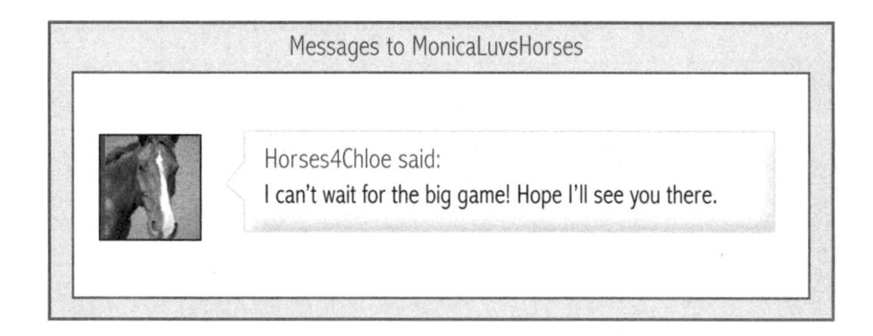
Messages to MonicaLuvsHorses

Horses4Chloe said:
I can't wait for the big game! Hope I'll see you there.

Chapter Eight

Official Substitute

All of my buttons were gone by the time I got to school on Thursday morning. Claudia and Becca had sold all their buttons, too.

We counted the money in homeroom.

"We have plenty of money for cider and doughnuts!" Becca exclaimed. "We can buy dozens and dozens."

"Good," Adam said. "I can eat a whole dozen by myself!"

"I'll bring the cider and doughnuts," Claudia said. "But I don't think there's enough money for napkins and cups."

"We can drink out of the carton," Tommy said, winking at Becca.

"Gross!" Becca said, shaking her head. "You can be so disgusting sometimes, Tommy!" But she smiled at him.

I raised my hand. "I'll bring napkins and cups. We have a billion at home."

Granite Electric, where Logan worked, ordered too many supplies for last year's company picnic. Logan brought some of the extra cups, plates, and napkins home to our house. He wouldn't mind if I took a few of them for me and my friends.

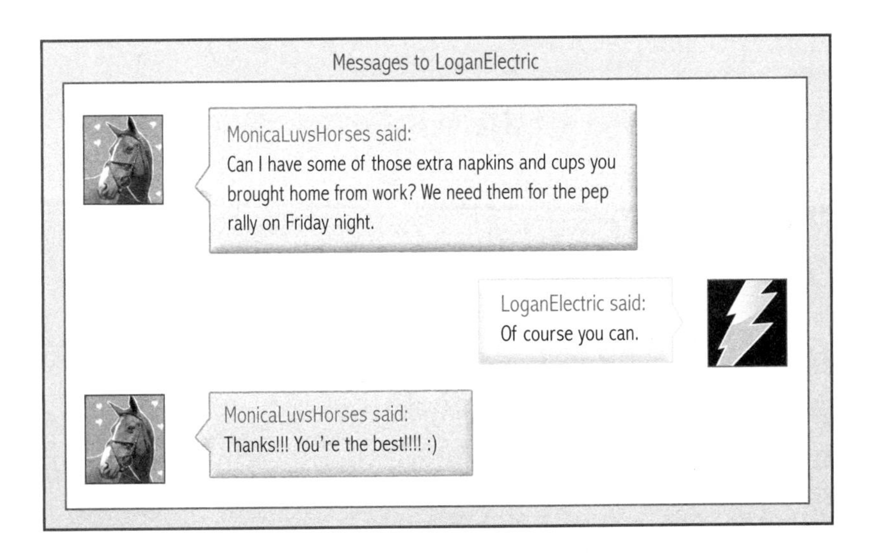

* * *

Our house was empty when I walked in after school.

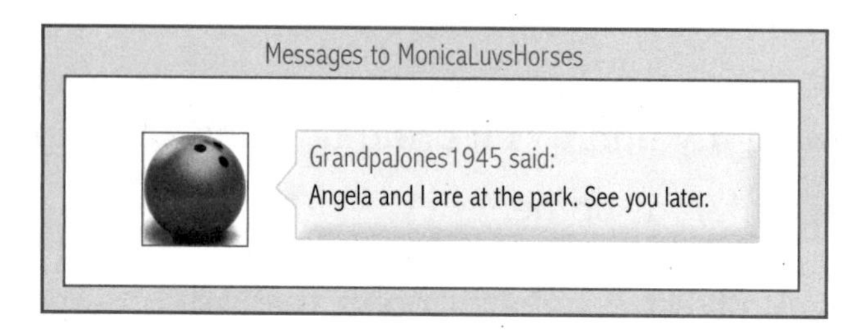

I couldn't believe it.

No Angela!

No cartoons!

No screeching fits!

Bliss!

I dropped my backpack, flopped on the sofa, and reached for the TV remote. I had a bunch of homework, but it could wait until after dinner.

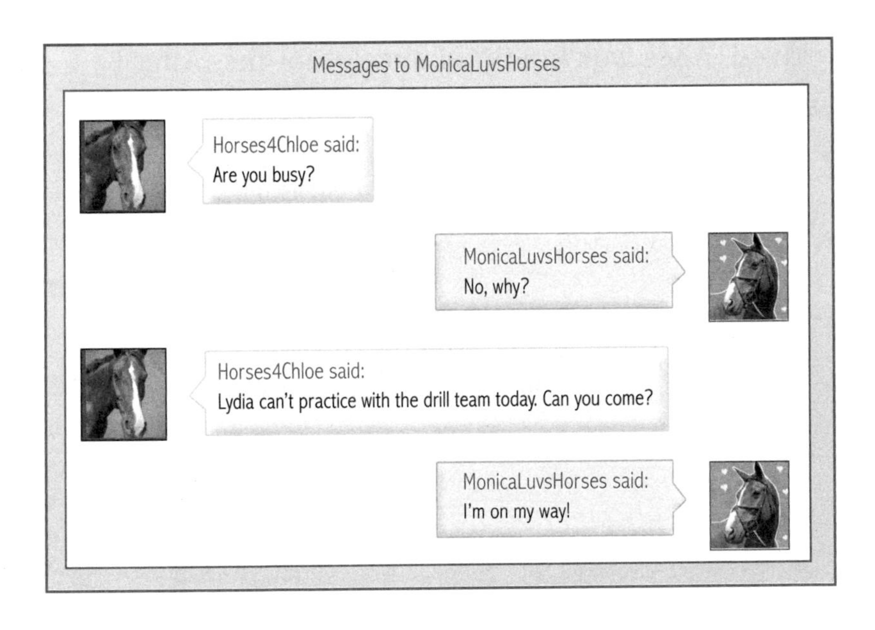
Messages to MonicaLuvsHorses
Horses4Chloe said:
Are you busy?
MonicaLuvsHorses said:
No, why?
Horses4Chloe said:
Lydia can't practice with the drill team today. Can you come?
MonicaLuvsHorses said:
I'm on my way!

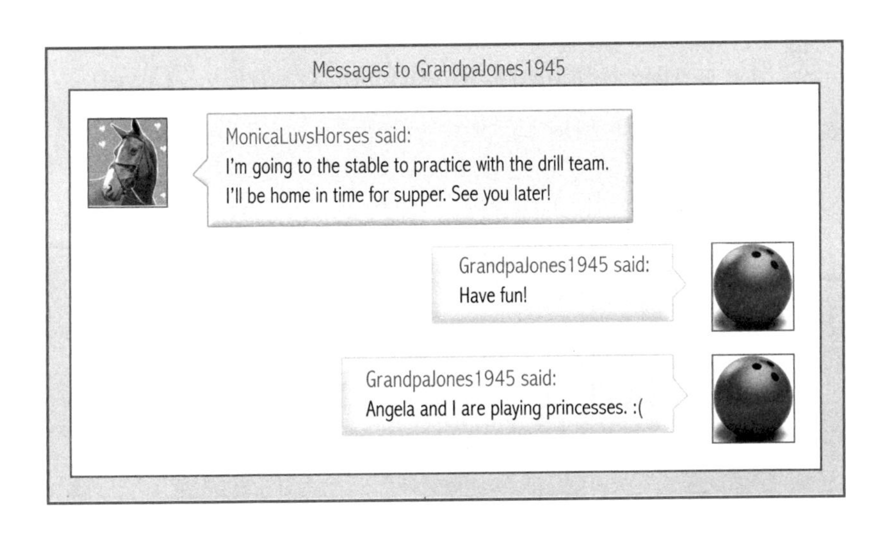
Messages to GrandpaJones1945
MonicaLuvsHorses said:
I'm going to the stable to practice with the drill team.
I'll be home in time for supper. See you later!
GrandpaJones1945 said:
Have fun!
GrandpaJones1945 said:
Angela and I are playing princesses. :(

Drill team practice had already started when I arrived. Alice was holding Lancelot for me. After I mounted, she called the team together.

"I have some bad news," Alice said. "The doctor won't let Lydia ride until Monday."

Alice's bad news was good and bad for me.

"You'll have to ride in the parade, Monica," Alice said.

I stared at her. I was too shocked to answer.

Megan gasped. "But Monica goes to Pine Tree!" she said.

"She wants her team to win on Saturday," Owen said. "She can't ride for Rock Creek."

"We need twelve riders," Rory said. "And Monica practiced with us all week. No one else knows the parade drills."

"I, uh — can't," I stammered. This might be my only chance to ride in a parade, but I couldn't miss the Pine Tree Pep Rally. "I have to be somewhere else on Friday night."

"What time?" Chloe asked.

"Eight," I said.

"Then there's no problem," Alice said. "The parade starts at six and runs about an hour."

"I'll take care of Lancelot when we're finished," Rory said. "That'll save time."

"You'll be home by 7:30," Alice added.

My mind raced. The Pine Tree Pep Rally started at 8. I had time to do both.

"You're the official Rock Creek Riders substitute," Chloe said. "You have to ride."

That cinched it.

"I'll be there," I said.

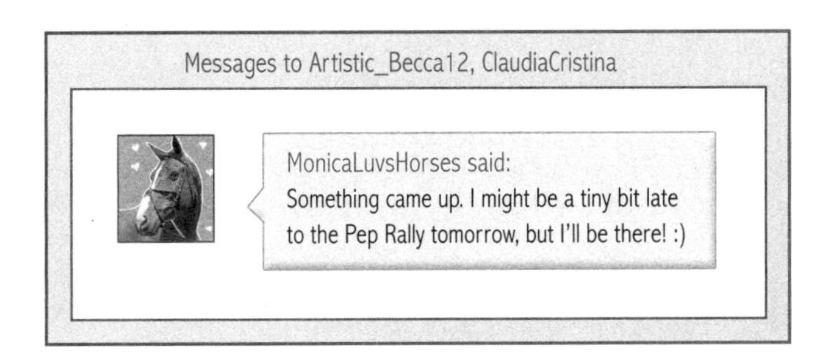

Chapter Nine

The Sneakiest Rider

I was so excited about riding in the Rock Creek Rally Parade, I couldn't sleep. I was also super stressed out.

The next morning, I made Mom, Logan, and Grandpa promise not to tell Angela about the Rock Creek parade.

"Angela will want to come," I explained. "And she'll want to wear Pine Tree colors. What if she boos the Bears at their own parade?"

Logan understood the problem. "That would be pretty embarrassing, wouldn't it?" he asked.

I nodded. "I'm riding to help my friends at the barn. I'm not rooting for Rock Creek," I explained.

"I'll take Angela to the Pine Tree Pep Rally," Grandpa said.

"She'll love that!" I said. "Everyone will think she's adorable in her cheerleading outfit."

Angela didn't see me drive off with Mom and Logan after school. She was in the backyard practicing her cheers.

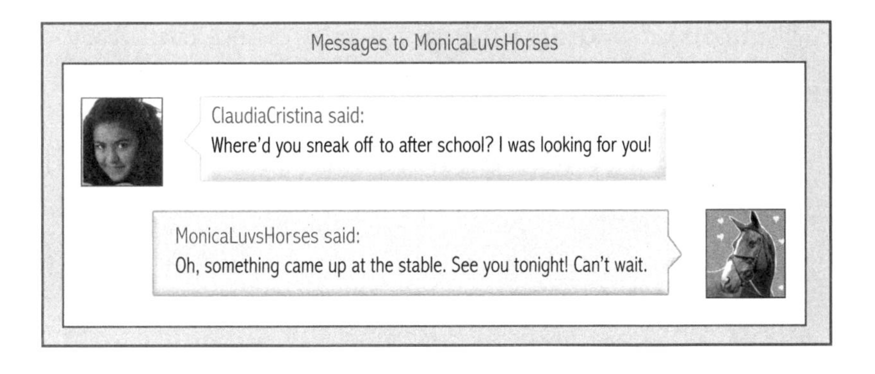

We drove straight to the field where the parade was lining up. Logan and Mom dropped me off. Then they left to find a good spot to watch the parade.

I found my group. "I'm so glad you're here!" Chloe said. "This is going to be so much fun."

I saddled Lancelot and took the reins. At the stable, I used a mounting block. I couldn't get on from the ground. Lancelot stood still, but he was very tall.

"I'll give you a leg up," Rory said.

"Thanks," I said, smiling. I bent my leg, and Rory gave me a boost.

The view was great from Lancelot's back. I watched everyone line up.

The mayor of Rock Creek sat in a red convertible car. He was first in line for the parade. The Rock Creek marching band was second. The Bears football team and cheerleaders were next.

Further back in the line, several school clubs had decorated floats. Other groups wore uniforms and carried banners.

I suddenly realized that the parade was a big deal. My stomach flip-flopped.

I looked at Chloe and Rory in a panic. "What if I make a huge mistake?" I asked nervously. "I'll mess up the whole team!"

"You won't make any mistakes," Chloe said.

Rory smiled. "I'm right in front of you. Just do what I do," he said calmly.

That made me feel better. Rory would be calling out the commands. I couldn't do anything wrong if I followed him.

The drill team was next to last in line. A hay wagon pulled by a tractor was behind us.

"How come we're so close to the end?" I asked Chloe.

"So that if one of the horses poops, no one will step in it," Chloe explained.

That made sense. But, I realized, it would take us longer to finish the route.

The parade started at 6:05.

The drill team didn't move until 6:25.

I stopped worrying about time the instant we started moving forward. I was riding a horse in a parade!

"You look great!" Alice called out.

I kept my eyes straight ahead, but I couldn't stop grinning. The team looked sharp, and I remembered everything I learned in practice.

The float in front of us stopped.

"Halt!" Rory ordered.

He waited until the float began to move. Then he called out, "Forward ho!"

We stopped and started our horses at exactly the same time. The people on the curb applauded.

Owen and Megan rode in the middle of the front line. Owen carried an American flag. Megan carried the Rock Creek Riders flag. When Rory called for a 2 x 2, each column had a flag. I could tell that we looked great.

Rory and Megan turned right. Chloe and I turned right behind them.

"Monica!" Mom shouted.

I spotted Mom and Logan waving in the crowd. I knew I couldn't wave back. I had to keep my hands on the reins. But I blurted out, "Hi, Mom!" and gave them a huge smile.

Chloe laughed. "I told you this was fun," she said.

"You were right," I said.

"Shhh!" Megan said. "Come on, Monica. Try to behave!" She shot us an annoyed look.

Rory glanced back and winked. Chloe saw, and she looked at me and raised her eyebrow. I just rolled my eyes and looked straight ahead.

Chloe thought I should have a **boyfriend.**

She thought Rory would be perfect. He was cute, and smart, and so nice. But I didn't want to lose him as a friend.

Both columns of horses joined back up. The parade marched down the main street and back up the next street over. We returned to the field at 7:36.

Mom and Logan were waiting there to take me home. "You were great!" Mom told me.

I slipped off Lancelot and handed the reins to Rory. "Are you sure you don't mind taking care of him?" I asked.

"No problem," Rory said. "Are you sure you don't want to go to Owen's party?"

"I'd love to, but I can't," I said. "Some other time," I added as I rushed off.

In the car, I wanted Logan to drive faster, but he said he couldn't speed. Then we hit every red light between Rock Creek and our house.

"We better hurry," I told Mom and Logan. "I'll change fast but I don't have time to shower. Can you grab the cups and napkins? And put them in the car, and make sure —"

"Calm down, Monica," Mom said. "I'm sure you won't be late."

It was 8:07 when I ran in the front door.

The Pep Rally had started

without me.

Chapter Ten

P-T-C-V, What's That Spell?

I was 33 minutes late when I finally got to the pep rally. I wandered through the crowd looking for my friends.

Bunches of kids were standing around tables or sat on blankets. Half of them had Cougar claws or pom-poms. Anna and Carly sat on canvas chairs by a striped tent. More kids formed a ring around the blazing bonfire.

The cheerleaders led them in a cheer.

"Go Pine Tree!
Go green!
Go Cougar gold,
go team!"

Everyone on the sidelines whistled and cheered.

I saw Claudia and ran over. "Sorry I'm late," I said.

"I'm just glad to see you," Claudia said. "I was afraid you weren't going to make it."

"You didn't answer your phone!" Becca said.

I patted my pockets. They were empty. "I must have left it in the car," I said. "I'm sorry."

Claudia had set up folding chairs and a card table for our refreshments. Tommy lifted a cider carton. He pretended to take a drink.

"Don't you dare do that, Tommy!" Becca yelled.

I held up my bags. "I have napkins and cups!"

"Saved!" Tommy exclaimed.

We put the napkins and cups on the table. A crowd gathered to get drinks and doughnuts.

"There's Monica!" Angela's shrill voice rang out. She marched up to me. "Where were you? We looked everywhere."

"Monica had things to do," Grandpa said.

"She smells funny." Angela crinkled her nose.

I winced, but no one else seemed to notice that I kind of smelled like a horse.

"Wow!" Adam said, smiling at Angela. "You look just like a cheerleader."

"I do?" Angela grinned. "I made up a cheer. Watch." She hopped up, jumped in place, and shook her pom-poms as she chanted.

"P is for Pine.
T is for Tree.
C is for Cougars.
And V is for victory!"

"Fantastic!" Becca said. She clapped and smiled at Angela.

"That was really good, Angela," Adam said. "You should show it to the Cougar cheerleaders."

Angela gasped. "Will they like it?" she asked nervously.

"Let's find out," Adam said. "Come with me."

The cheerleaders took a break, and music blared from the loudspeakers. Several kids started dancing.

Peter ran over from the science club group. "I just heard some great news. Adam is going to play tomorrow," he told us.

"Are you sure?" I asked. Peter was very smart, and he was almost always right. But Adam wasn't the best half-back on the team. "We're playing for a spot in the state championship game," I reminded Peter.

"Is Coach Johnson really going to use second-string players?" Becca asked.

"He said, 'Everyone who practiced gets to play.'" Peter lowered his voice to sound like Coach.

"That's only fair," Claudia said. "Adam would love to make a touchdown just once."

Just then, Adam came back without Angela and Grandpa. "Where's my sister?" I asked.

"Anna adopted Angela," Adam explained. "The squad loves her cheer."

I wasn't surprised. I knew Angela would fit right in with Anna and her friends.

Sylvia Slother and Larry Kyle walked over to our table. Larry grabbed a doughnut. "You wouldn't believe how many people are wearing your Cougars buttons," he said.

"Monica isn't," Sylvia said.

I slapped my hand to my chest. I had kept one button for myself. But I changed so fast after the parade I forgot to put it on!

"Monica sold all her buttons," Claudia said.

"Oh," Sylvia said. She chewed her doughnut very slowly. "Too bad she forgot to keep one."

I rolled my eyes and turned away.

My friends and I ate doughnut and hotdogs, sipped cider, talked, and laughed at Tommy's jokes. Some of them were even funny.

"What state does a football player like best?" Tommy asked.

Becca shrugged. "I don't know," she said.

"New Jersey." Tommy cracked up.

I looked at Adam. "I don't get it."

"Football shirts are called jerseys," Adam explained.

I groaned. "Good one, Tommy," I said.

When the rally was over, everyone helped Claudia pack. Becca, Adam, and I made sure all the mess was picked up. I was supposed to ride home with Angela and Grandpa. I didn't have my phone, so I couldn't call or text Grandpa. I kept looking for them, but they didn't show up. Anna and Carly did.

"Angela fell asleep," Anna told me. "Your grandpa took her to the car."

"Thanks, Anna." I smiled. "And thanks for being so nice to my sister."

"She's cute," Anna said. "And she's not a Rock Creek fan like you are, Monica."

"What does that mean?" Claudia asked.

"Carly and I went to the Rock Creek parade to spy," Anna said. "Monica was riding in their parade!"

She yelled the last sentence. A bunch of kids who were walking by stopped and stared at me.

Becca gasped. "Is that why you were late, Monica?" she asked.

I nodded. I was too upset to talk.

Our class bully, Jenny Pinski, was never too upset to talk. She blasted me. "You jinxed Pine Tree, Monica! If we lose tomorrow, it will be your fault."

My friends wouldn't look at me.

I knew what they thought. I was a traitor.

Chapter Eleven

Just This Once

Grandpa knew something was wrong when I got into the car. "Are you okay, Monica?" he asked.

"Yeah," I said.

"No, she's not," Angela said from the back seat. "She's a traitor."

"Who told you that, Angela?" Grandpa asked.

"Anna." Angela smiled sweetly. "She likes me even though my sister is a traitor."

I didn't care what Anna thought. I was miserable because my friends were mad at me. And it was my fault. I had ridden in the Rock Creek parade.

* * *

I was still miserable when Grandpa, Angela, and I left for the game Saturday afternoon. My friends were waiting by the bleachers, just as we planned.

"You're late, Monica," Tommy said. "We almost sat down without you."

"I wasn't sure you wanted to sit with me," I said quietly. I was wearing my Cougars Rule button. I hoped it would help.

Claudia stepped forward. "We don't believe you're rooting for Rock Creek," she said.

"I'm not," I said.

"But you rode in their parade," Becca added.

"I had to," I said. "Lydia usually rides on the drill team, but she was sick all week so I practiced with them because they need twelve riders." I paused to take a breath. "She was supposed to be better by Friday, but she wasn't, so I had to ride in the parade. I'm the official Rock Creek Riders substitute."

"Horses," Adam said. "Is that excuse good enough this time?" he asked our friends.

Everyone made faces like they were thinking about whether they'd ever like me again. I couldn't tell if they were teasing me, but I was starting to think they weren't mad anymore.

"Owen had a party after the parade," I told them, "but I didn't go, even though Rory asked me, because I didn't want to miss the Pine Tree rally."

Becca gasped. "You turned down a party with Rory?" she asked.

"That proves it." Claudia grinned. "Monica must be a loyal Cougars fan."

"Let's go, guys. It's almost kick-off time," Peter said.

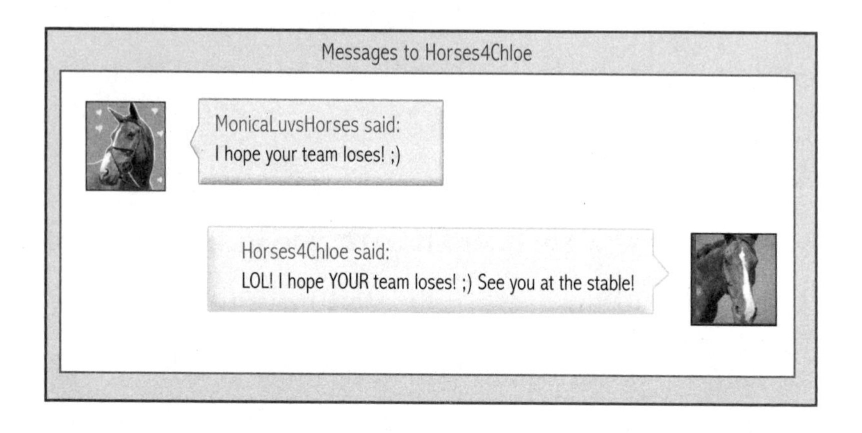

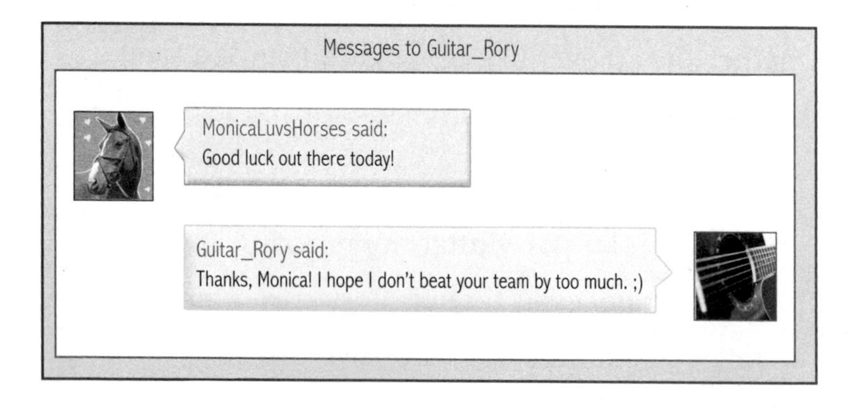

Grandpa and Angela had gone ahead to save seats. My friends and I sat down just as the teams ran onto the field.

"There's Brad!" Claudia yelled. She jumped up. "Go get 'em, Brad!"

Becca looked at me and giggled. Then she scooted over to make room for Tommy. I was pretty sure Claudia and Becca's secret crushes weren't all that secret.

We all cheered when we saw Adam. He looked up into the stands and waved at us.

Then I spotted Rory and yelled, "Yay, Rory!"

"Monica, are you waving to a Rock Creek guy?" Tommy asked.

I covered my mouth. Becca and Claudia both laughed.

"Rory is so cute and so nice we don't blame you," Becca said. "You can root for Rory."

"Just this once," Claudia added with a big smile.

My smile was bigger. My friends weren't mad me. I almost didn't care who won.

But Angela would be heartbroken if the Cougars lost. She shook her pom-poms and jumped up and down. When the cheerleaders used her cheer, she shrieked so much her voice cracked.

"I wrote that one!" Angela announced loudly.

When Rory kicked off to Pine Tree, I sprang to my feet, clapped, and shouted, "Go, Cougars!"

Messages to Guitar_Rory

MonicaLuvsHorses said:
You were great today.

Guitar_Rory said:
Thanks. :) It was cool to know you were watching.

Saturday, 11:30 p.m.

So the big Pine Tree-Rock Creek game was today. It was a great game! I couldn't believe how well Adam and Rory both played. Of course, in the end, only one team could win, and I think it was the team who played the best.

Watching the game was fun, but the best part was afterward. My friends and I all went to to the Pizza Palace, and we stayed for hours, ordering more pizzas when we felt like it, drinking gallons of soda, laughing, and talking.

I love my Pine Tree friends. Since I was so busy practicing for the Rock Creek parade, I haven't had a lot of time to spend with them.

So tonight was awesome.

Of course, I love my friends from the stable too. Rory and Chloe are amazing!

I just wish they all could be friends. My dream is to get all of them together so they realize how cool they all are. Then we could be one huge group of friends! It would be INCREDIBLE!

I think I drank too much soda. I won't be able to go to sleep for HOURS.

Maybe I'll sneak downstairs and see if there's anything good on TV.

love,

Monica

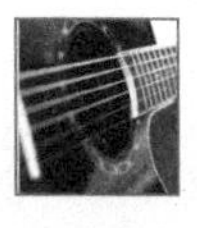

1 comment from Rory: I wish I could've been at the Pizza Palace with you. Sounds fun. We'll have to do that after your lesson sometime.

Leave a comment:

Name (required)

FRIEND BOOK

Wall | Info | Photos | Notes

View Photos of Me (100)

Edit My Profile

My Friends (236)

INFORMATION:

Relationship Status:
Single

Astrological Sign:
Taurus

Current City:
Pine Tree

Family Members:
Traci Gregory
Logan Gregory
Frank Jones
Angela Gregory

Best Friends:
Claudia Cortez
Becca McDougal
Chloe Granger
Adam Locke
Rory Weber
Tommy Patterson
Peter Wiggins

MONICA MURRAY

AVATAR

SCREEN NAME: MonicaLuvsHorses

ABOUT ME:

Activities: HORSEBACK RIDING!, hanging out with my friends, watching TV, listening to music, writing, shopping, sleeping in on weekends, swimming, watching movies . . . all the usual stuff

Favorite music: Tornado, Bad Dog, Haley Hover

Favorite books: A Tree Grows in Brooklyn, Harry Potter, Diary of Anne Frank, Phantom High

Favorite movies: Heartbreak High, Alien Hunter, Canyon Stallion

Favorite TV shows: Musical Idol, MyWorld, Boutique TV, Island

Fan of: Pine Tree Cougars, Rock Creek Stables, Pizza Palace, Red Brick Inn, K Brand Jeans, Miss Magazine, The Pinecone Press, Horse Newsletter Quarterly, Teen Scene, Boutique Magazine, Haley Hover

Groups: Peter for President!!!, Bring Back T-Shirt Tuesday, I Listen to WHCR In The Morning, Laughing Makes Everything Better!, I Have A Stepsister, Ms. Stark's Homeroom, Princess Patsy Is Annoying!, Haley Should Have Won on Musical Idol!, Pine Tree Eighth Grade, Mr. Monroe is the Best Science Teacher of All Time

Quotes: No hour of life is wasted that is spent in the saddle. ~Winston Churchill

A horse is worth more than riches. ~Spanish proverb

arch rivals (ARCH RYE-vuhlz)—enemies

arena (uh-REE-nuh)—a large area that is used for sports or entertainment

breeches (BRICH-iz)—knee-length pants that are tight at the bottom

bribe (BRIBE)—money that is offered to someone to get them to do what you want them to do

drill team (DRILL TEEM)—a group of riders who perform routines

exhibition (ek-suh-BISH-uhn)—a public performance

formation (for-MAY-shuhn)—the ways in which the members of a group are arranged

loyal (LOI-uhl)—firm in faithfulness

official (uh-FISH-uhl)—approved

patient (PAY-shuhnt)—good at putting up with problems without getting upset

permanent (PUR-muh-nuhnt)—lasting forever

souvenir (soo-vuh-NEER)—an object you keep to remind you of a place, event, or person

TEXT 911!

With your friends, help solve these problems.

Messages to Text 911!

1

MonicaLuvsHorses said:
What should I do if I feel torn between two different groups?

Messages to Text 911!

2

ClaudiaChristina said:
My friend forgot about some plans we had. What should I do?

Messages to Text 911!

3

Angela said:
My big sister never lets me hang out with her. How can I make her play with me?

You can write too.

Some people write in journals or diaries. I have a secret blog. Here are some writing prompts to help you write your own blog or diary entries.

1. I rode in my first parade. Write about something you just did for the first time. What was it? How did you feel afterward?

2. I have two groups of friends, but Claudia is my best friend. Write about your best friend.

3. The big game between Rock Creek and Pine Tree was a lot of fun. Write about a fun event that took place at your school.

ABOUT THE AUTHOR: DIANA G. GALLAGHER

Just like Monica, Diana G. Gallagher has loved riding horses since she was a little girl. And like Becca, she is an artist. Like Claudia, she often babysits little kids — usually her grandchildren. Diana has wanted to be a writer since she was twelve, and she has written dozens of books, including the Claudia Cristina Cortez series. She lives in Florida with her husband, five dogs, three cats, and one cranky parrot.

CLAUDIA CRISTINA CORTEZ and Monica

More Stories about Best Friends

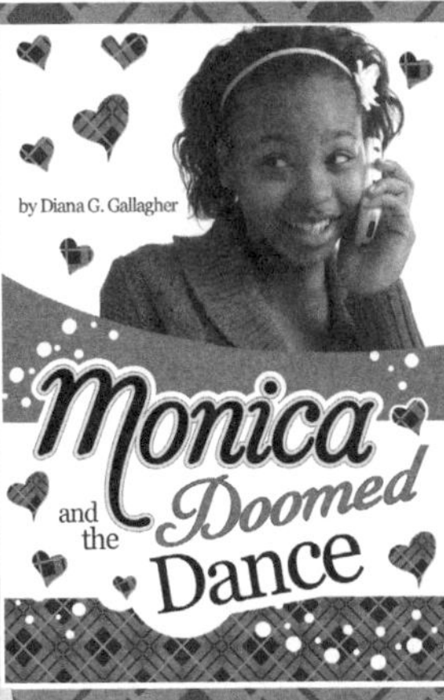

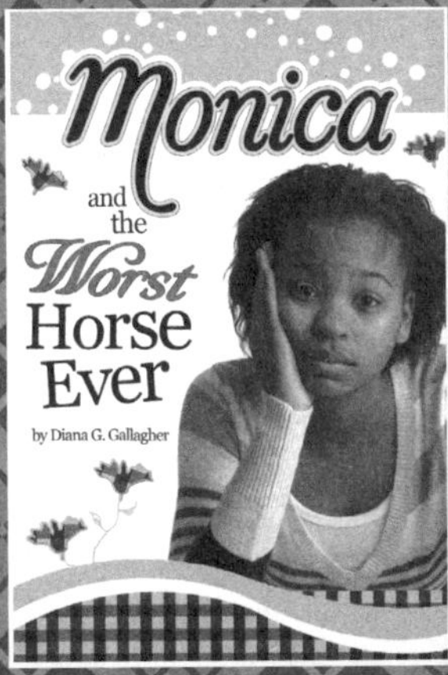

WAIT!
DON'T close the book!
There's
MORE!
FIND MORE:
Games
Puzzles
Heroes
Villains
Authors
Illustrators at...
www.
capstonekids
.com
Just type in the Book ID: 9781434219831
and you're ready to go!
Still want more?
Find cool websites and more books
like this one at www.Facthound.com.